McGoogan Moves the Mighty Rock

for Eleanor Connell Schena

Dick Gackenbach

McGoogan Moves the Mighty Rock

Harper & Row, Publishers

imself, McGoogan, Master Guitar Player and Singer of Songs, stepped out of the blistering sun and into the cool shadow of a mighty rock.

"Ah, 'tis a fine spot to have a bite to eat," he said. "And a place to rest me weary bones, as well."

Himself took a seat and opened his sack. He spread out his hard rolls and soft cheese with the manners of a prince. His appetite was good and McGoogan ate quickly. Then he leaned back against the rock and patted his belly.

"Me belly's full and me mind's at peace," he said with a sigh. "Now, 'tis time to feed me spirit."

McGoogan picked up his guitar and plucked it gently. He sang a song he made up himself.

"Beautiful mermaid, answer for me,
who put the salt in the briny sea?
Did you, ladyfish,
because they ate your sister
from a steamin' dish?
Was it you, me darlin',
that put the salt in the sea?"

"BRAVO! WELL DONE!" a voice cried out.

"Sure and I thought I was alone," said the startled McGoogan.

He got up from his seat in the shade and ran around the rock.

"There's not another soul about," McGoogan said. "Except for meself and this fine rock!"

"Sing another song about the sea," the voice said again.

McGoogan stepped back and took a long hard look at the rock.

"Now I wonder," he said, smiling all over.
"Might I be conversin' with a talkin' rock?"

"I'm delighted you heard me," said the rock.
"Most people do not."

"Well, me boyo," said McGoogan, "there's
some that never listen. As for me," he said, "I've
traveled all over makin' me poor livin' singin'
songs. And in me time, I've heard everything.
I've listened to the winds cry, and the ships sing
as they sail. I've heard the chatter of the
dolphins and the bellowin' of the whales, I
have." Then McGoogan tipped his hat. "Now, 'tis
me pleasure to make the acquaintance of a
rock."

"Thank you," replied the rock. "You say you travel, do you?" it asked McGoogan.

"I do," answered McGoogan, as he returned to his seat in the shade.

"It must be wonderful," said the rock. "Moving about from place to place, I mean."

"Ay, I'm happy on the move," replied McGoogan.

"Tell me about your travels," said the rock eagerly.

McGoogan leaned back and scratched his head. "Well," he began, "I've seen a land where trees grow tall as mountains!"

"Imagine that," said the rock.

"And I've seen people," McGoogan continued, "who grow no taller than a bush!"

"I envy you," confessed the rock. "I've never been anywhere, you see."

"I'm sorry for ya, poor divil," said McGoogan.

"You are kind," said the rock. "But please go on."

"I'm not braggin', ya understand," McGoogan continued. "But I've been to a land where there's no water atall. A desert, they call it."

"A desert! Think of that!" exclaimed the rock.

"And there's water, too," McGoogan said, "without a bit of land for thousands of miles about."

"I KNOW THAT," cried the rock with such excitement the earth trembled. "THAT'S THE SEA!"

McGoogan jumped to his feet. "How would you know? You, that's never moved an inch?" he demanded to know.

"From other men who sat in my shade," the rock calmly told him. "I listened to the tales they told each other about the wonders of the sea. Tales of pearls, and awesome storms, and fish with tiger jaws. Is it any wonder, then, I dream of going to the sea myself someday?"

"Ha," laughed McGoogan. "You've as much chance of goin' to the sea as I have of livin' in a palace and keepin' me toes warm in winter."

"Is that your dream?" asked the rock. "To live in a palace?"

"Ay." McGoogan chuckled. " 'Tis one of them."

"In that case," said the rock, "you can have a palace. And I can go to the sea."

"You'd be sproutin' wings and flyin', I suppose?" McGoogan waved his arms like a bird.

"Don't be silly," replied the rock. "*You* will take me to the sea."

McGoogan gave the rock a terrible look. "Not on yer life!" he bellowed. "Why should I break me back takin' you to the sea?"

"For gold!" said the rock.

"For gold, is it?" McGoogan's eyes opened wide.

"For a nugget the size of your fist," said the rock.

"And where would you be gettin' such a nugget?" McGoogan wanted to know.

"I have one within me," the rock confided. "I'll give it to you, if you take me to the sea."

"Within you?" said McGoogan. "But how would I get it?"

"Trust me," said the rock.

"Ah," grumbled McGoogan. "Ya strike too hard a bargain. Takin' the likes of you to the sea would be an awful task."

"But it could be done," insisted the rock.

"It could," McGoogan reluctantly agreed. "But think of the snags. Think of the donkey work I'd be askin' for."

"Think of the gold," suggested the rock.

"Ay," said McGoogan. "That's a lot of gold."

"You could buy a palace," said the rock.

"That I could," said McGoogan thoughtfully.

"You could have a wife like a queen," added the rock.

McGoogan nodded. And for a while he said nothing. He paced up and down in front of the rock.

Then McGoogan snapped his fingers and danced a jig.

"I'll do it," he cried. "For that much gold, I'd carry me mean cousin Charley back from the divil's own gate.

"Besides," McGoogan told the rock, "I like ya. I fancy the pleasure of yer company on the way to the sea. When would ya like to go?"

"The sooner the better," the rock shouted with joy.

"Today it is," McGoogan decided then and there.

Himself took an axe
from his sack and went to
a nearby woods.
When he returned, McGoogan
carried two logs. One log
he placed at the base
of the rock for a wedge.
The other log
he used for a lever.

"We're off, ya big bogey," shouted McGoogan, pushing down on the lever. Slowly, very slowly, McGoogan and the rock moved toward the sea.

The days that followed were hot and hard on
McGoogan. On uphill days they seldom moved
ahead more than a foot or two.

But on downhill days the pace
was swift and easy.

The nights were cool, and very peaceful.
McGoogan and the rock sat beneath the stars
and warmed themselves before a roaring fire.

"Sing for me," the rock would ask each night.

And so McGoogan did, with great delight. He
sang his songs to the rock while the fire made
the shadows dance. For Himself, McGoogan, had
never had a finer audience than his friend, the
rock.

One morning, soon after their day's journey had begun, McGoogan and the rock met a farmer on the road.

"I've been looking for stone to build a well," the farmer told McGoogan. "May I have some from this fine rock you have?"

McGoogan excused himself and ran around to the opposite side of the rock. "He wants a bit of you to build his well," McGoogan whispered to the rock.

"Is a well a good thing?" the rock asked.

"It is," McGoogan said.

"Then let the farmer take some stone from me," the rock said.

Later, when they camped for the night, McGoogan put his hand gently on the rock. "Did the chippin' hurt atall, when the farmer took his stone?"

"No, I didn't feel a thing," the rock told him.

"I'm glad for that," said McGoogan.

Each day of their journey was a joy for the rock. There were new things to see it had never seen before. But for McGoogan, one day was like another, up one hill and down the next. Himself rarely took a rest, except when more men halted their journey in search of stone.

"We need stone for steps," they would say. Or, "We need stone to build a bridge."

Each time men begged for stone, McGoogan talked the matter over with the rock. "Is it a good thing they wish to build?" was all the rock ever wanted to know. If McGoogan said it was, the men got their stone. If he said it wasn't, no stone was given.

Once, a man with an empty cart demanded McGoogan give him stone to build a fence.

"And what would you be wantin' a fence for?" McGoogan asked the man.

"Why, for keeping some fools in," replied the man, "and for keeping other fools out."

McGoogan whispered to the rock, "No stone for him."

"No stone," agreed the rock.

But when the reasons were good, the rock was generous. McGoogan watched each day while his friend gave away stone for many things on the way to the sea. Grindstones, millstones, whetstones, and milestones. Even a tombstone when needed.

Finally, one night as the two friends sat by the fire, McGoogan reached over and touched the rock.

"Ya know," he announced, "you've been so generous, yer no more than a mere stone yerself now."

"Am I still a burden?" asked the rock.

"Yer no trouble atall," McGoogan answered softly. Then he picked up his guitar and sang songs to the rock until it was time to fall asleep.

Bright and early next morning, they awoke. Large white birds were flying in the sky above them.

"Look!" shouted McGoogan. "We must be near the shore."

"Don't tease me, McGoogan," said the rock.

"Would I do that?" said McGoogan. "Those are sea gulls flying there," he said, pointing to the birds. "And sea gulls live by the edge of the sea!"

"Glory be, at last!" cried the rock.

Without wasting any time, McGoogan picked up the rock and tucked it under his arm.

"Let's go," he said. "The sea cannot be far away."

"Hurry," the rock cheered him on.

McGoogan walked briskly, saying nothing except to answer his friend's endless question.

"Soon?" the rock asked time and time again.

"Soon!" McGoogan answered, patting the rock each time.

Suddenly, McGoogan stopped and sniffed the air. "That's salt in the wind," he said, "or I'm no son of Erin."

Then he saw the dunes ahead.

"Hold on," McGoogan cried. He ran, holding
the rock tightly to him. He ran up and over the
dunes and down across the white sandy beach.
He stopped when he reached the water's edge.

"There, me fine bucko," Himself bellowed in
triumph. "There is your sea."

The rock was enchanted. "It is a sight beyond
my wildest dream."

Together, they watched the sea a long time
without saying a word.

The rock spoke first. "McGoogan," it said, "the nugget of gold is just beneath my shell. Take it! It belongs to you now."

"Ya mean break ya open? No," said McGoogan. "I don't want it. Ya mean more to me than any fistful of gold."

"But what about your palace?" the rock asked.

"The divil take the palace," said McGoogan.

"What about your wife like a queen?" asked the rock.

"She'd only be wantin' me money," said McGoogan. "I'll find me a lass that loves me for what I am."

"You are a wonder," said the rock. "And full of gold yourself."

"Go on with ya now." McGoogan laughed.

"Nevertheless," said the rock sadly, "I'm sorry our journey has ended."

"Ended, has it?" said McGoogan. "There's more to see than just an ocean. Don't ya recall me tellin' ya about trees growin' big as mountains? And men no taller than a bush?"

"I remember," said the rock.

"Well then," McGoogan said with a smile, "give me the pleasure of showin' them to ya. What d'ya say?"

"Oh, me darlin' friend," cried the rock. "I'd love to go travelin' with the likes of you."

So off they went, Himself, McGoogan, and Nugget of Gold, Big As Your Fist. All the way, laughing with the pebbles and singing to the rocks, and having a grand old time.

McGoogan Moves the Mighty Rock
Copyright © 1981 by Dick Gackenbach
First Edition

Library of Congress Cataloging in Publication Data
Gackenbach, Dick.
    McGoogan moves the mighty rock.

    SUMMARY: McGoogan, Master Guitar Player and Singer
of Songs, befriends a rock with a hankering to see the
sea.
    [1. Rocks—Fiction.   2. Friendship—Fiction]
I. Title.
PZ7.G117Mac 1981   [E]   80-8455
ISBN 0-06-021967-X
ISBN 0-06-021968-8 (lib. bdg.)